A Lift-the-Flap Book

The C Santa Surprise

For Alex Jarvis

Suzy-Jane Tanner

HarperFestival®
A Division of HarperCollinsPublishers

It's Christmas Eve!

Santa is delivering presents to the last children on his list.

Oh no, the children
are coming!
Quick, Santa, hide!

Here are the presents.
What do you think
Charlie's present is?

Charlie

Can you guess what Jenny's present is?

What did Santa bring for Lucy?

Here's a present for Billy. What could it be?

Here's a present
for Santa.
But where can he be?

"A present for me?
I wonder what it is."

Merry Christmas, everyone!

The End